This book is dedicated to our spirited princesses Catherine, Alexandra, Danika, Emmalynn, and Megan. May you follow your heavenly Father's words and fulfill His will for your life. Just never lose your princess panache!

To our knights in shining armor, Bruce and Ralph; thank you for sharing our vision for our heritage. We love you and are blessed to "run the race" with you!

J.Y. and J.J.

Dedicated to my father . . .

O.A.

ZONDERKIDZ

Princess Grace and the Little Lost Kitten
Copyright © 2011 by Jeanna Young and Jacqueline Johnson
Illustrations © 2011 by Omar Aranda

Requests for information should be addressed to:
Zonderkidz, 3900 *Sparks Dr. SE*, Grand Rapids, Michigan 49546

Library of Congress Cataloging-in-Publication Data
Young, Jeanna Stolle, 1968-
    Princess Grace and the little lost kitten / by Jeanna Stolle Young and
Jacqueline Kinney Johnson ; [illustrations by Omar Aranda].
       p. cm.
    Summary: When young Princess Grace cannot find one of the kittens she
promised to care for, the King sends all of his daughters and his best riders far
and wide to seek the lost one in this version of the parable of the lost sheep.
Includes note about the parable and its meaning for children.
    ISBN 978-0-310-71640-2 (hardcover)
    [1. Princesses—Fiction. 2. Cats—Fiction. 3. Animals—Infancy—Fiction. 4. Lost
and found possessions—Fiction. 5. Christian life—Fiction. 6. Parables.] I. Johnson,
Jacqueline Kinney, 1943- II. Aranda, Omar, ill. III. Title.
PZ7.Y8654Prg 2011
[E]—dc22
                                       2010002001

Editor: Mary Hassinger
Art direction & design: Kris Nelson
Illustrator: Omar Aranda/The Illustrators Agency

Printed in China

15 16 17 18 19 20 21 22 / LPC / 22 21 20 19 18 17 16 15 14 13 12 11 10 9 8 7 6

The Princess Parables

Princess Grace
and the Little Lost Kitten

WRITTEN BY **Jeanna Young** & **Jacqueline Johnson**
ILLUSTRATED BY **Omar Aranda**

ZONDER**kidz**

Once upon a time, in a magnificent castle perched high on a hill above the sea, there lived five princesses and their father, a gentle and loving king. Their names were Grace, Joy, Faith, Charity, and Hope. They were blessed to be daughters of the king.

This is the story of Princess Grace. She is full of adventure and fills her days with drama and activity. If there is no plan, she will make one. She is never bored and when she finds herself with a few moments, she will most definitely get into trouble!

One evening, Princess Grace slid down the banister on her way to dinner, knocking over a vase of fresh-cut flowers. Quickly cleaning up her mess, she heard rustling noises from the stairwell closet and decided to investigate. She slowly opened the door and crept inside to take a look.

In the darkness of the corner, Grace saw five fluffy faces looking up at her. She squealed in surprise and slowly knelt beside them, lovingly stroking each tiny purring face. One kitten jumped up, stepping on all the others, to get her attention. "Aren't you the curious one?" Princess Grace giggled.

Hearing her squeal, Grace's sisters and father appeared in the doorway. "What have we here?" the king asked.

"Daddy, Daddy, may we please keep them?" shouted Princess Grace.

"Well, I don't know," the king answered. "Let's talk about it over dinner."

As Princess Grace took her seat, the curious kitten sprang out of her arms onto the dining room table. Knocking over the cream pitcher, taking two quick licks, she leapt over the tiered cake prepared for dessert. Colored icing and cream footprints were now everywhere. The king asked with a raised eyebrow, "Who will make sure these kittens won't get into any trouble?"

Princess Grace enthusiastically raised both hands. "I will feed them and play with them," she said. "I promise! I will do a good job."

The king said, "I am counting on you, Grace."

Grace picked up her kitten, mess and all. "I will name you Poppy, for you popped into my life with your trouble-making ways."

Each morning the princesses ran down the castle steps into the kitchen to scoop up their special new friends. The girls dressed the kittens in doll clothes. They played with them in their castle playhouse.

One day while playing a game of hide-and-seek, Poppy bolted for the door onto a freshly cleaned and still-wet stone floor. Much to her surprise, she slid all the way down the hallway, like a bowling ball on a slippery lane. Poppy slammed right into the king's feet. Laughing, the king picked up the jostled kitten, hugged her, and sent her on her way!

One morning Princess Grace called the kittens into the kitchen for breakfast. She counted them as they came running: one … two … three … four … but Poppy wasn't there. Grace called again, but the adventurous kitten did not come. Where could she be?

Poppy was lost!

In a panic, Princess Grace began to search the castle. "Daddy is relying on me," she thought. "I must find Poppy! She will be cold, afraid, and hungry with nothing to eat!"

After scouring every inch of the castle and grounds, Grace burst into tears. The king found her in distress and gently comforted her. Through her tears, Grace explained that her kitten had vanished. "We must find Poppy. Will you help, please?"

Grace was overjoyed and humbled by her father's quick actions. He sent for her sisters, his best horses, and his most trusted riders to go with her. The king explained lovingly to all the princesses, "You are each important to me, even when you get into trouble. Search everywhere for our lost kitten. Bring her back safely to the castle. Go now with my blessing."

Princess Grace and her sisters headed swiftly on horseback toward the meadowlands. They searched the town and countryside. They asked storekeepers, merchants, and farmers if they had seen a lost kitten. They rode to the ocean and asked the ship captains and crews if Poppy was a stowaway onboard their boats.

"Don't give up," said Princess Charity, reassuringly. "We will find Poppy. Our father would not give up, and neither will we."

Soon the princesses came upon the Black Woods. The five princesses looked at each other. What should they do? They had never been in the dark forest. Then they remembered what their father had told them. "Search everywhere for the lost kitten. Bring her back safely to the castle."

The sisters led their horses slowly and bravely into the Black Woods. The princesses heard wolves howling in the distance. They felt huge spiderwebs brush against their faces and arms. They saw dark shadows move on their left and right. But the sisters moved steadily forward. They called and listened for Poppy's tiny meow. They peered through the gloom, searching the shadows for any sign of the lost kitten. Princess Hope took Grace's hand and held it tightly.

Princess Grace's throat felt so tight that she couldn't call out. The silence was heavy around her. She almost gave up. Grace whispered a prayer for help and took a step forward.

Just then, she tripped on a log and fell to the wet ground. Flustered, she lifted her head and found herself face-to-face with a drenched and almost unrecognizable Poppy. She was rumpled and a bit messy, but she looked unharmed!

Princess Grace wrapped the wet kitten in her cape next to her heart while they rode swiftly home to the warm castle.

The king joyfully greeted the girls and led them into the ballroom for a huge feast and a special dish of cream for Poppy.

Around the fireplace that night, the king and his daughters enjoyed bread pudding smothered in sweet cream. The princesses told of the daring adventure they had while searching for Poppy. But now they were thrilled to be home, safe and together again.

Parable Thoughts

My name is Grace. My name means "favor" or "blessing." God blesses me with the strength and desire to do what is right, even in times of trouble. I had to be brave to go into the Black Woods, but I did it because that one trouble-making, adventurous little kitten was important to me, just as you and I are important to God. All of God's creatures are worthy of love and protection, especially the ones that are lost or get into trouble! God will come after us, just like I went after Poppy. It is the lost ones that he came to save.

My story is like a story in the Bible. You can find the parable Jesus told in Matthew 18:12–14. Our heavenly Father looks for the one sheep that is lost and brings that one to the safety of his kingdom. Just as my sisters and I sat by the fire in the safety of the castle with our father, the king, you too can be found and safe in the care of the one true King.

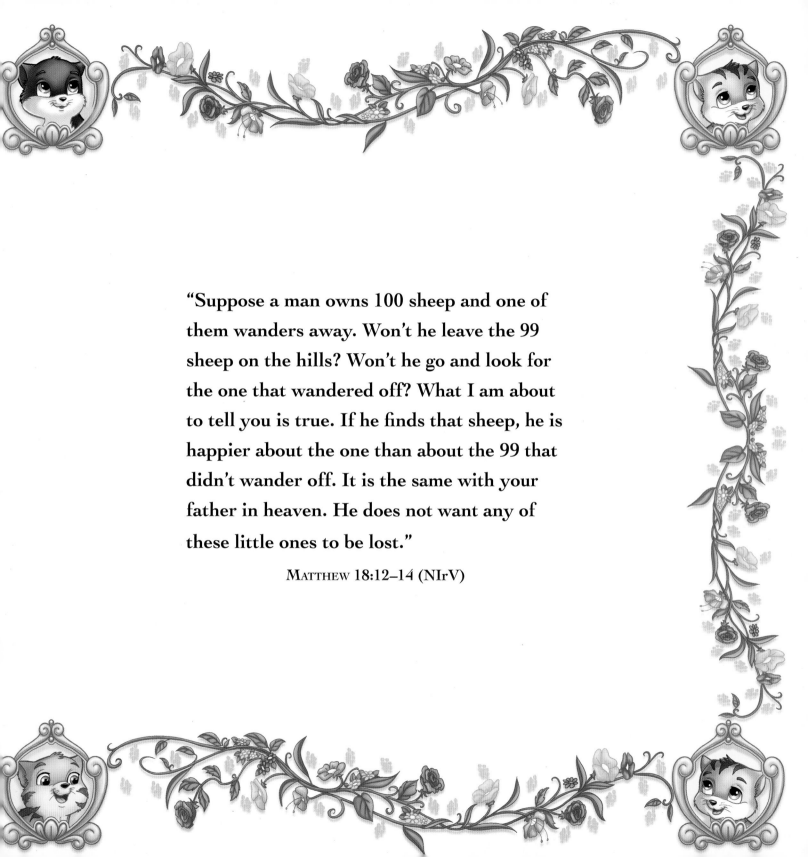

"Suppose a man owns 100 sheep and one of them wanders away. Won't he leave the 99 sheep on the hills? Won't he go and look for the one that wandered off? What I am about to tell you is true. If he finds that sheep, he is happier about the one than about the 99 that didn't wander off. It is the same with your father in heaven. He does not want any of these little ones to be lost."

Matthew 18:12–14 (NIrV)